ESTEBAN
and the Ghost

ESTEBAN
and the Ghost

adapted by Sibyl Hancock · pictures by Dirk Zimmer

Dial Books for Young Readers

E. P. Dutton, Inc.

NEW YORK

E

For Britt, Brian, and Kevin—never a dull moment!
S. H.

For Thea
D. Z.

Published by Dial Books for Young Readers
A Division of E. P. Dutton, Inc.
2 Park Avenue
New York, New York 10016

Typography by Jane Byers Bierhorst
Printed in Hong Kong by South China Printing Co.
First Edition
10 9 8 7 6 5 4 3 2 1

Library of Congress Cataloging in Publication Data

Hancock, Sibyl. Esteban and the ghost.

Summary: Esteban, a merry Spanish tinker, spends All Hallows' Eve
in a haunted castle and helps a ghost win his way into heaven.
[1. Ghosts—Fiction. 2. Spain—Fiction. 3. Halloween—Fiction.]
I. Zimmer, Dirk, ill. II. Title.
PZ7.H1916Es 1983   [E]   82-22125
ISBN 0-8037-2443-8   ISBN 0-8037-2411-X (lib. bdg.)

Esteban and the Ghost *is adapted from "The Tinker and*
the Ghost" in Three Golden Oranges *by Ralph Steele Boggs*
and Mary Gould Davis, copyright 1936 by Longmans, Green and Co.
by permission of David McKay Co., Inc.

The art consists of black line-drawings and full-color washes.
The black line is prepared and photographed separately for greater
contrast and sharpness. The full-color washes are prepared with
watercolor on the reverse side of the black line-drawing.
They are then camera-separated and reproduced as red, blue, yellow, and black halftones.

Long ago late in October a merry tinker named Esteban came to a village near Toledo. It was All Hallows' Eve, and he had heard a tale that excited him to no end. Nestled in the golden hills of Spain stood a dark dwelling called Gray Castle, and it was said to be haunted.

As Esteban sat about mending pots and pans for the village housewives, he asked if the ghost story was true.

"Yes, indeed," one wife said. "You can hear the moaning and weeping in the castle every night."

"And on All Hallows' Eve a ghostly light flickers in the chimney," added another. "The owner of the castle has offered a thousand gold reales to anyone who can drive the ghost away. Brave men have tried but each has been found dead, sitting before the fireplace in the morning."

Esteban chuckled, for he was delighted by the task. "Dear ladies, I, Esteban, am afraid of nothing. I should like to sleep tonight in this castle. Perhaps I can keep the poor ghost company, and it will not weep so loudly."

The women were amazed as Esteban bid them good day. He rode his donkey to the marketplace and bought a slab of bacon, a dozen eggs, a good frying pan, a jug of tart apple cider, and some firewood. With his donkey laden with supplies Esteban set out for the castle.

The night was windy and cold when Esteban reached the castle courtyard. Leaving his donkey to graze by a pool overgrown with weeds, he carried his firewood and food into the great hall.

"It's so dark in here, I cannot see my hand before me," Esteban said. And the sound of his voice sent bats flapping from the rafters.

"That is much better," he said, starting a fire in the huge fireplace. "Nothing like a bright fire to drive away fear."

Esteban sliced some bacon, placed it in the skillet, and set it over the flames. How it sizzled in the pan! Just as he was about to take a sip of cider, a sad voice wailed down the chimney.

"*Oh, me!*" it cried. "*Oh, my! Oh, me!*"

"That's not a very happy greeting, good fellow," Esteban said as he turned his bacon over.

"But then I am one who is used to hearing the donkey braying, and perhaps your voice is not so bad after all."

"*Oh, me!*" cried the voice. "*Oh, my! Oh, me!*" The thin moaning echoed through the great hall.

Esteban lifted the crisp bacon from the sizzling grease and laid it on some paper to drain. Then he broke an egg into the skillet. He carefully jiggled the pan so that the egg would be soft in the middle, for that was how he liked his eggs.

"*Look out below!*" the voice cried out again, sounding shaky and frightened. "*I'm falling!*"

"Very well," Esteban said calmly. "But see that you don't land in my frying pan."

There was a loud bump, and on the fireplace hearth lay a man's leg! And a fine leg it was, too, clothed in a half pair of blue woolen trousers and a shiny black boot.

Esteban ate his bacon and egg and drank some of his tart cider. Outside the castle the rain pounded the aged gray stones, and the wind howled about the corners of the towers.

Suddenly the voice wailed once more, *"Look out below! I'm falling!"*

There was another thump, and a second leg lay on the hearth. It looked just like the first leg.

Esteban stared thoughtfully at the second leg for a moment, then pulled it farther away from the fireplace. He stacked on more wood and broke another egg into the frying pan.

"Look out below!" yelled the voice, sounding no longer weak but quite loud. *"I'm falling!"*

"Go right ahead," Esteban said happily. "Just don't land in my egg."

With a very loud bump the trunk of a man's body lay on the hearth, and it was wearing a fine blue woolen coat with a red checkered shirt.

Esteban thought the ghost was quite well-dressed and proceeded to cook his third egg and some more bacon. He was just finishing the last of the bacon when the voice cried out once again. First one arm fell down the chimney and then another.

"Well, now," Esteban murmured softly. "All that's left is the head. I'd like to see what the fellow looks like."

Esteban did not have long to wait.

"LOOK OUT BELOW!" the voice boomed. "I'M FALLING!"

And a handsome head, with dark curly hair and a beard, rolled onto the hearth.

Esteban watched as the parts of the body joined together.

Brave though he was, he gave a startled gasp when a tall
husky man stood up—looking not at all like a ghost.

"Welcome," Esteban said, after he had gathered his wits.
"Would you care for some food?"

"It is not food I want," the ghost replied. "Out of all those who have come to the castle, you are the only man brave enough to stay until I could put myself back together again. The others died of pure terror before I was even halfway finished."

"Indeed." Esteban sighed, stirring the flames higher in the fireplace. "That is because I brought good food and warmth to keep me company. And I had no cause to fear you."

"Please," begged the ghost, "if you will help me again, you may save my soul. In the courtyard under a tree, I once buried three bags filled with copper, silver, and gold coins, which I had stolen from some thieves."

"Why, that makes you a thief too!" Esteban exclaimed. "A robber of robbers!"

"I am that," the ghost admitted sadly. "Alas, I had no sooner hidden the coins than the thieves found me and killed me. Those thieves were devilish-mean, cutting my body to pieces.

"They never did find the coins. You must dig them up. Give the copper coins to the church, the silver to the poor of the village, and keep the gold for yourself. Do this for me, and I can at last enter the Kingdom of Heaven."

Esteban felt sorry for the ghost, so he followed him into the courtyard to one of the trees.

"This is the place," the ghost said. "Dig."

"Not unless you help." The big fellow might be a ghost, Esteban thought, but he could handle a shovel as well as any man.

So together they dug while the wind and rain beat against them. Yet, they found nothing.

"It is not here!" the ghost wailed. "Alas, I do not remember which tree it was." And he threw back his head and howled.

"Oooo-oooooh! I must find the money now!

"What hour is it?" the ghost screeched.

Esteban pulled out his pocket watch. "Fifteen minutes before the stroke of twelve."

"If we do not find the coins right away, I will be doomed to haunt this castle—the scene of my crooked deed— forever," the ghost cried.

"Saint Peter himself decreed that I should have exactly fifty years to undo my crime and win my way into Heaven. Tonight at midnight my time will run out. He also commanded that whoever aided me must share my sorry lot. You, too, my friend, will be doomed for eternity."

"*I?*" Esteban looked at the ghost and wondered if the fateful words were true. "Why did you not tell me sooner?"

"For fear you would not help me," the ghost explained in a wavering voice. "Although I am able to return to the earth every All Hallows' Eve, without your aid I could never have put myself together again.

"Now, dig!" he commanded as best he could.

"Humph!" Esteban snorted. "At last I can see your dishonest ways for myself. I am angry enough to take a good swing at you, even though you are a ghost."

Esteban raised his fists and stepped forward.

"Pray, don't hit me," the ghost moaned, cringing. "I might fly into pieces again."

With an effort Esteban regained his temper, but his heart was pounding. "No amount of money is worth chancing a doomed soul," he muttered, thinking bitterly of his reward. "Let us hurry and try another tree."

By the time they had dug around the third tree, the ghost howled so loudly, Esteban felt a shiver creep up his spine. Time was fast running out.

"OOOO—OOOOOOH!"

The ghost's eyes were growing wild with panic.

"Will you stop that awful noise!" Esteban said sharply. "If we but had the light of the moon to see by."

"Moon!" the ghost cried. "Now I remember. I buried the money by the tree at the edge of the garden pool. The moon was shining on the water."

In no time they had unearthed the three bags of coins.

"Do you promise you will do all that I told you?" asked the ghost.

"I will," said Esteban. "You may be a rascal, but you have my word."

In a flash the ghost disappeared, leaving his clothes lying empty on the ground. When Esteban heard the faint tolling of a bell he knew the ghost had entered Heaven. And not a moment too soon, for the witching hour was at hand.

Early the next morning the villagers came to Gray Castle expecting to discover yet another man sitting dead before the fireplace. Instead, they found Esteban whistling cheerfully, as he loaded the bags of coins on his donkey's back.

"You are alive?" they asked, not believing what they saw.
"I am that." Esteban laughed. "Alive as can be! The ghost is gone, and you will find his clothes in the courtyard.

"I shall go now and collect my reward from the castle's owner."

With that Esteban rode away from the shocked village people and soon collected his thousand gold reales from the grateful lord of the castle. He faithfully gave the copper coins to the church and the silver to the poor. With the reales and the bag of gold coins, Esteban lived happily for many years, still mending pots and pans from time to time.

And he never saw another ghost again.